D1532775

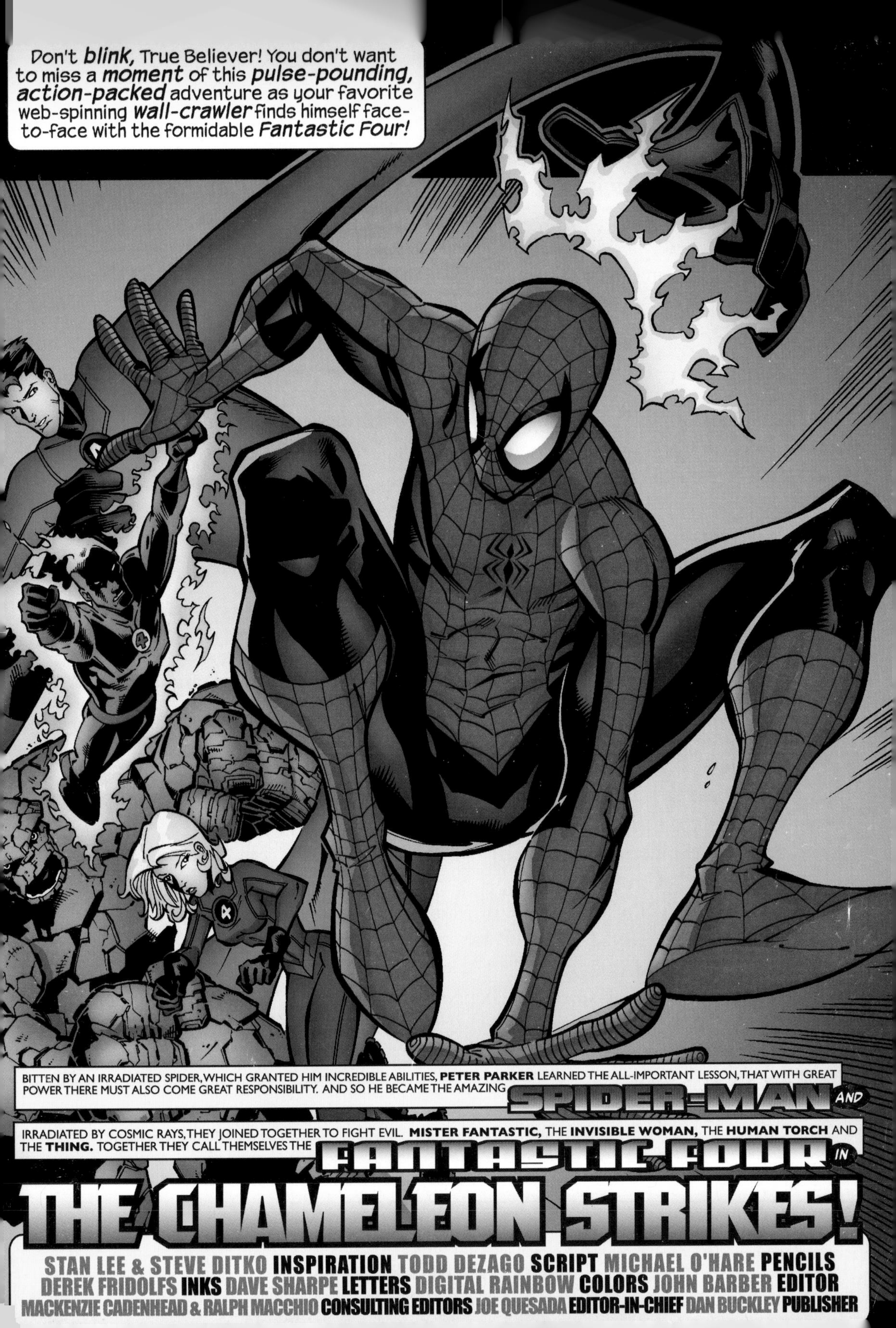
Don't blink, True Believer! You don't want to miss a moment of this pulse-pounding, action-packed adventure as your favorite web-spinning wall-crawler finds himself face-to-face with the formidable Fantastic Four!
BITTEN BY AN IRRADIATED SPIDER, WHICH GRANTED HIM INCREDIBLE ABILITIES, PETER PARKER LEARNED THE ALL-IMPORTANT LESSON, THAT WITH GREAT POWER THERE MUST ALSO COME GREAT RESPONSIBILITY. AND SO HE BECAME THE AMAZING SPIDER-MAN AND
IRRADIATED BY COSMIC RAYS, THEY JOINED TOGETHER TO FIGHT EVIL. MISTER FANTASTIC, THE INVISIBLE WOMAN, THE HUMAN TORCH AND THE THING. TOGETHER THEY CALL THEMSELVES THE FANTASTIC FOUR IN
THE CHAMELEON STRIKES!
STAN LEE & STEVE DITKO INSPIRATION TODD DEZAGO SCRIPT MICHAEL O'HARE PENCILS DEREK FRIDOLFS INKS DAVE SHARPE LETTERS DIGITAL RAINBOW COLORS JOHN BARBER EDITOR MACKENZIE CADENHEAD & RALPH MACCHIO CONSULTING EDITORS JOE QUESADA EDITOR-IN-CHIEF DAN BUCKLEY PUBLISHER

VISIT US AT
www.abdopublishing.com

Spotlight, a division of ABDO Publishing Company Inc., is the school and library distributor of the Marvel Entertainment books.

Library bound edition © 2006

Library of Congress Cataloging-in-Publication Data

Dezago, Todd.
   The chameleon strikes! / Stan Lee & Steve Ditko, inspiration ; Todd Dezago, script ; Michael O'Hare, pencils ; Derek Fridolfs, inks ; Dave Sharpe, letters ; Digital Rainbow, colors. -- Library bound ed.
       p. cm. -- (Spider-Man team up)
   "Marvel age"--Cover.
   Revision of the Nov. 2004 issue of Marvel age Spider-Man.
   ISBN-13: 978-1-59961-005-4
   ISBN-10: 1-59961-005-1
   1. Graphic novels. I. O'Hare, Michael (Michael S.) II. Marvel age Spider-Man. III. Title. IV. Title: Chameleon strikes! V. Series.

PN6728.S6D484 2006
741.5'973--dc22

2006043959

All Spotlight books are reinforced library binding and manufactured in the United States of America.

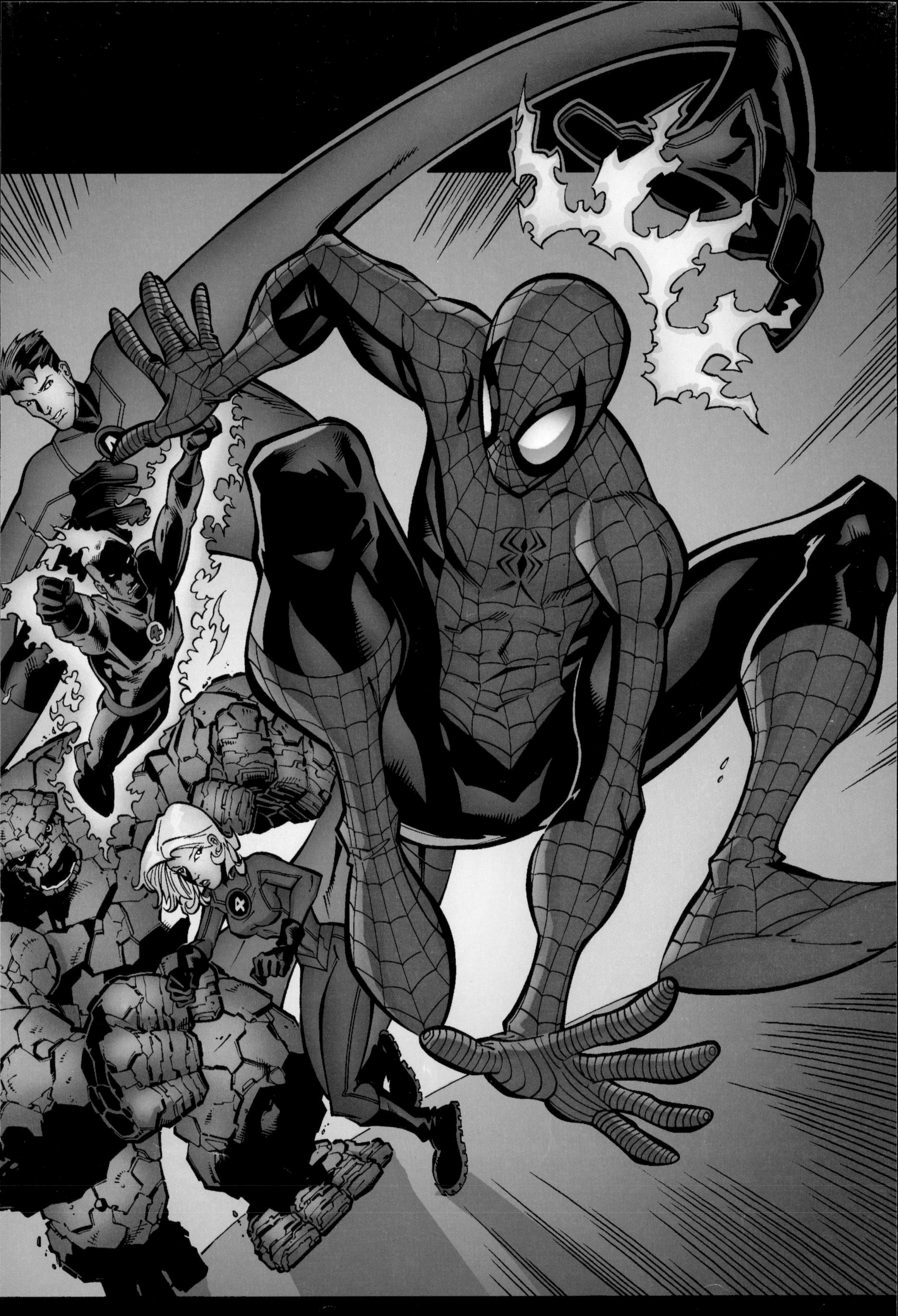

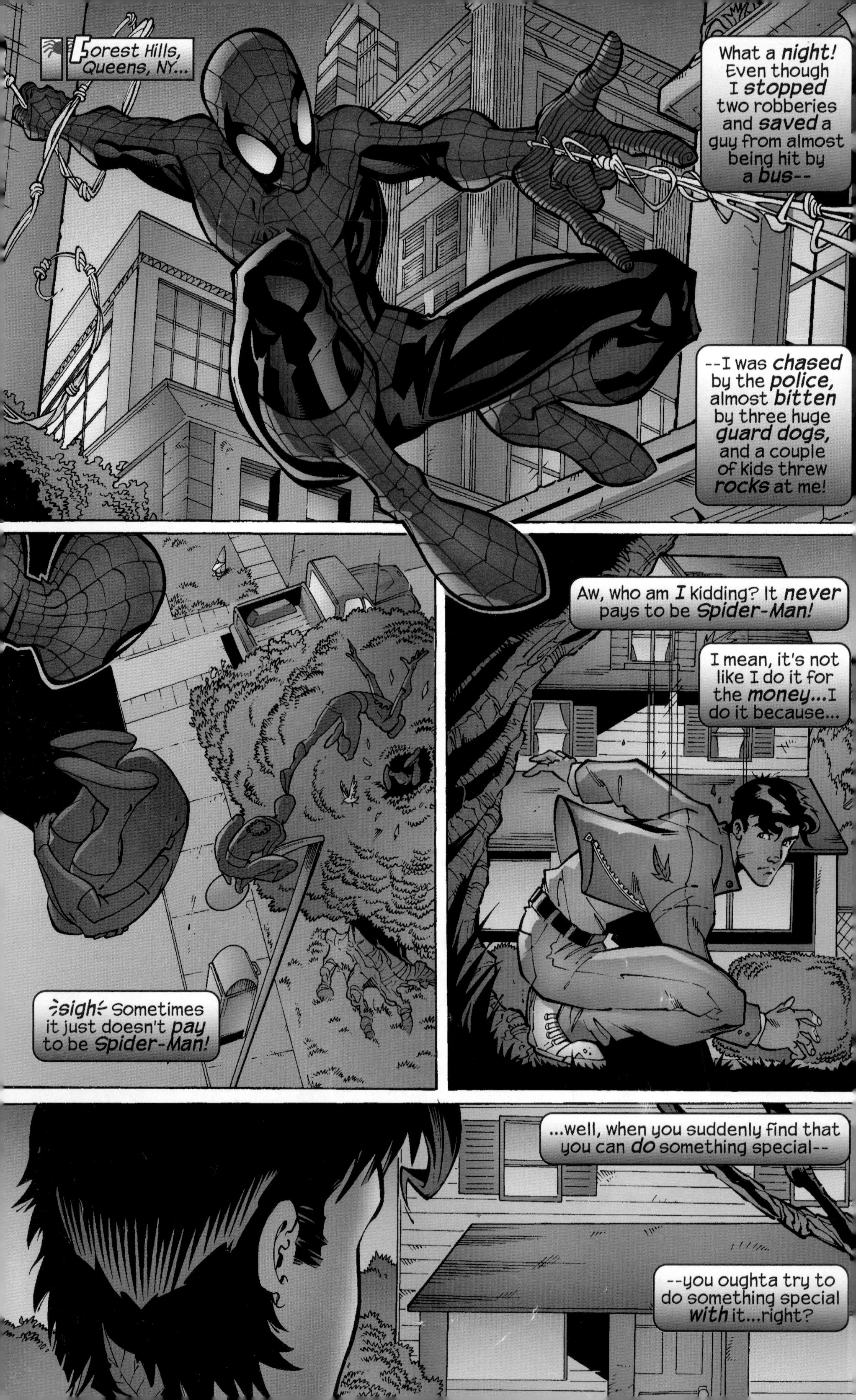
Forest Hills, Queens, NY...
What a night! Even though I stopped two robberies and saved a guy from almost being hit by a bus--
--I was chased by the police, almost bitten by three huge guard dogs, and a couple of kids threw rocks at me!
sigh Sometimes it just doesn't pay to be Spider-Man!
Aw, who am I kidding? It never pays to be Spider-Man!
I mean, it's not like I do it for the money...I do it because...
...well, when you suddenly find that you can do something special--
--you oughta try to do something special with it...right?

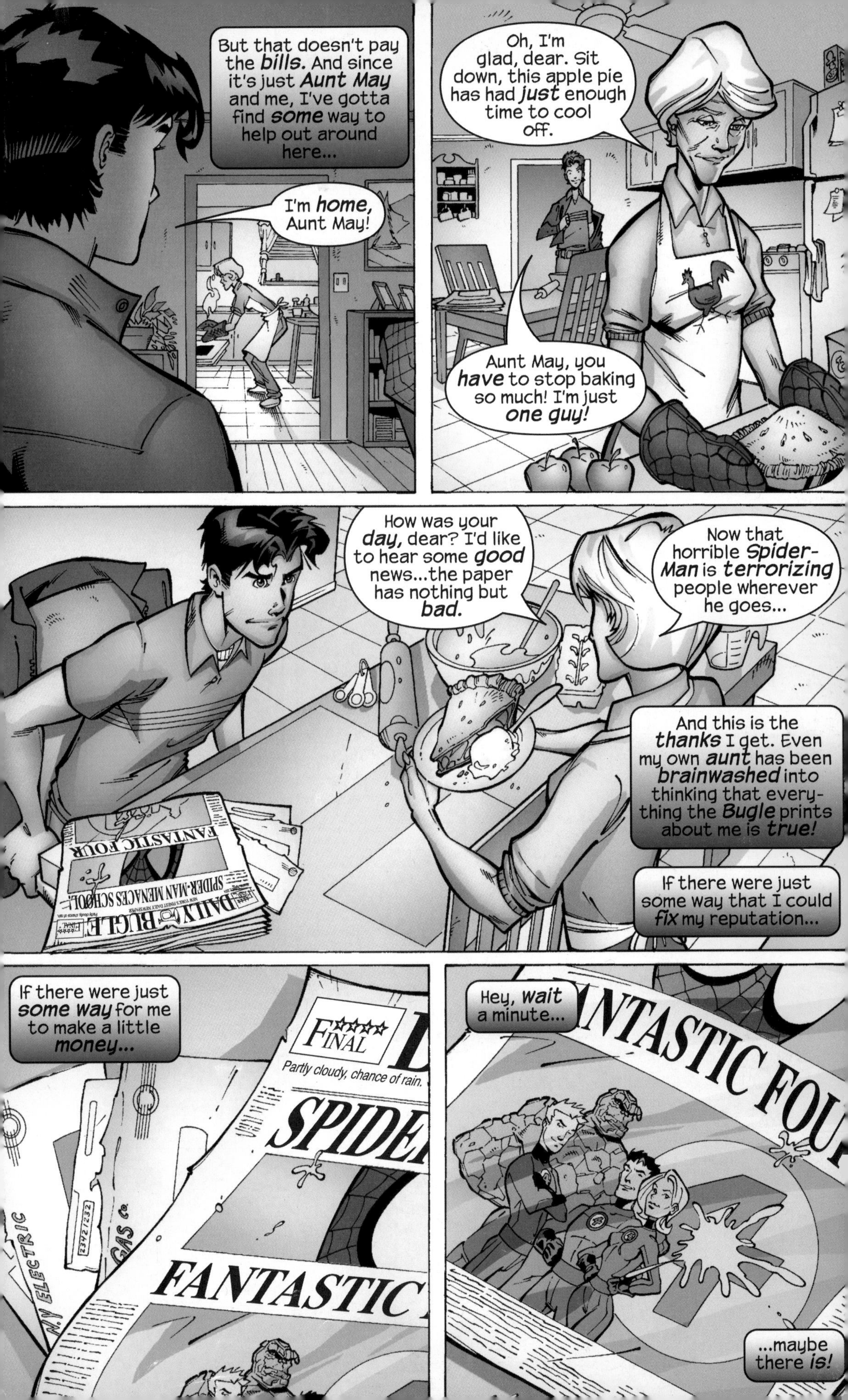
But that doesn't pay the bills. And since it's just Aunt May and me, I've gotta find some way to help out around here...
I'm home, Aunt May!
Oh, I'm glad, dear. Sit down, this apple pie has had just enough time to cool off.
Aunt May, you have to stop baking so much! I'm just one guy!
How was your day, dear? I'd like to hear some good news...the paper has nothing but bad.
Now that horrible Spider-Man is terrorizing people wherever he goes...
And this is the thanks I get. Even my own aunt has been brainwashed into thinking that every-thing the Bugle prints about me is true!
If there were just some way that I could fix my reputation...
DAILY BUGLE
SPIDER-MAN MENACES SCHOOL
FANTASTIC FOUR
If there were just some way for me to make a little money...
FINAL
Partly cloudy, chance of rain.
SPIDER
FANTASTIC
N.Y. ELECTRIC
GAS Co.
Hey, wait a minute...
NTASTIC FOU
...maybe there is!

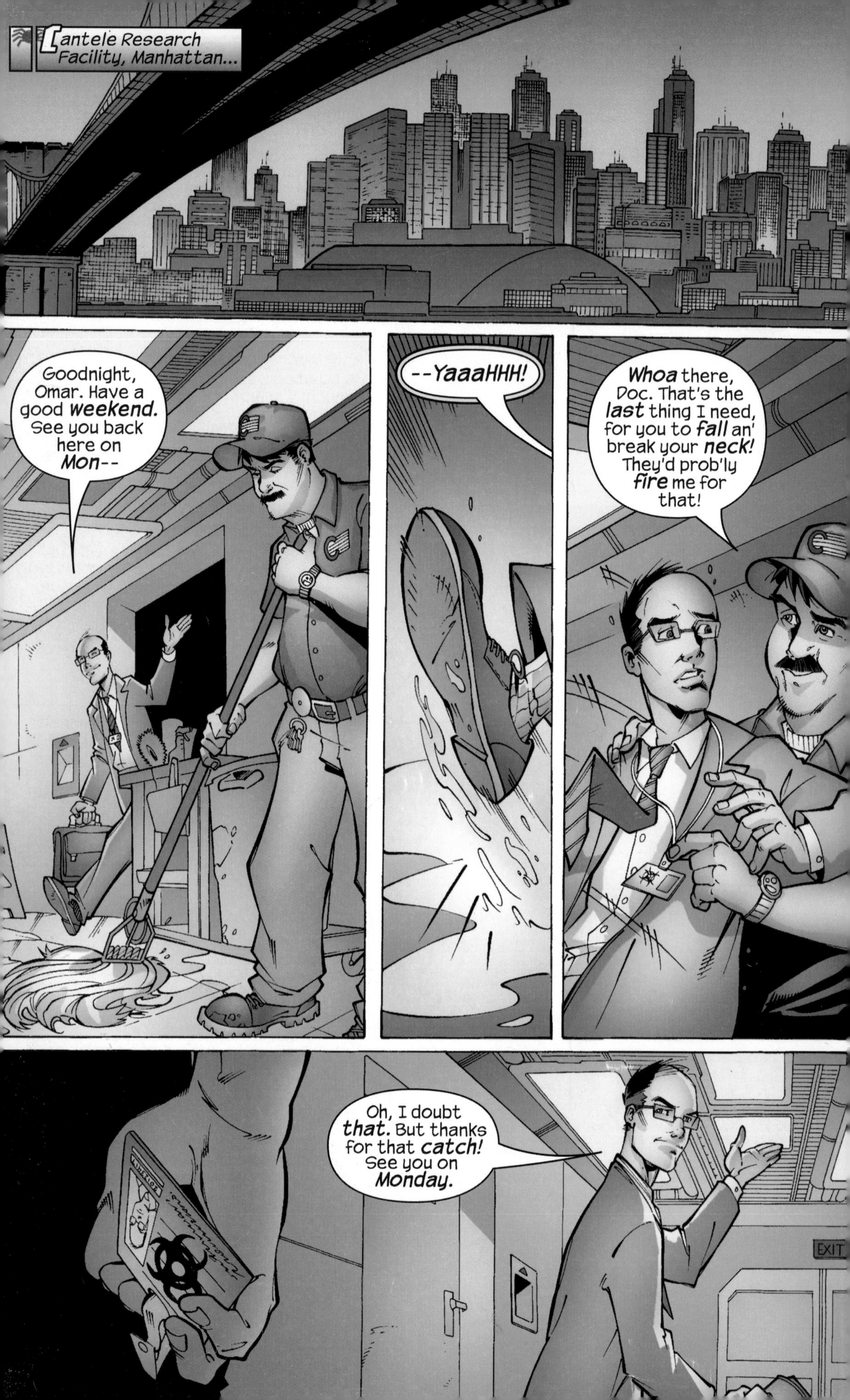

Cantele Research Facility, Manhattan...
Goodnight, Omar. Have a good weekend. See you back here on Mon--
--YaaaHHH!
Whoa there, Doc. That's the last thing I need, for you to fall an' break your neck! They'd prob'ly fire me for that!
Oh, I doubt that. But thanks for that catch! See you on Monday.
EXIT

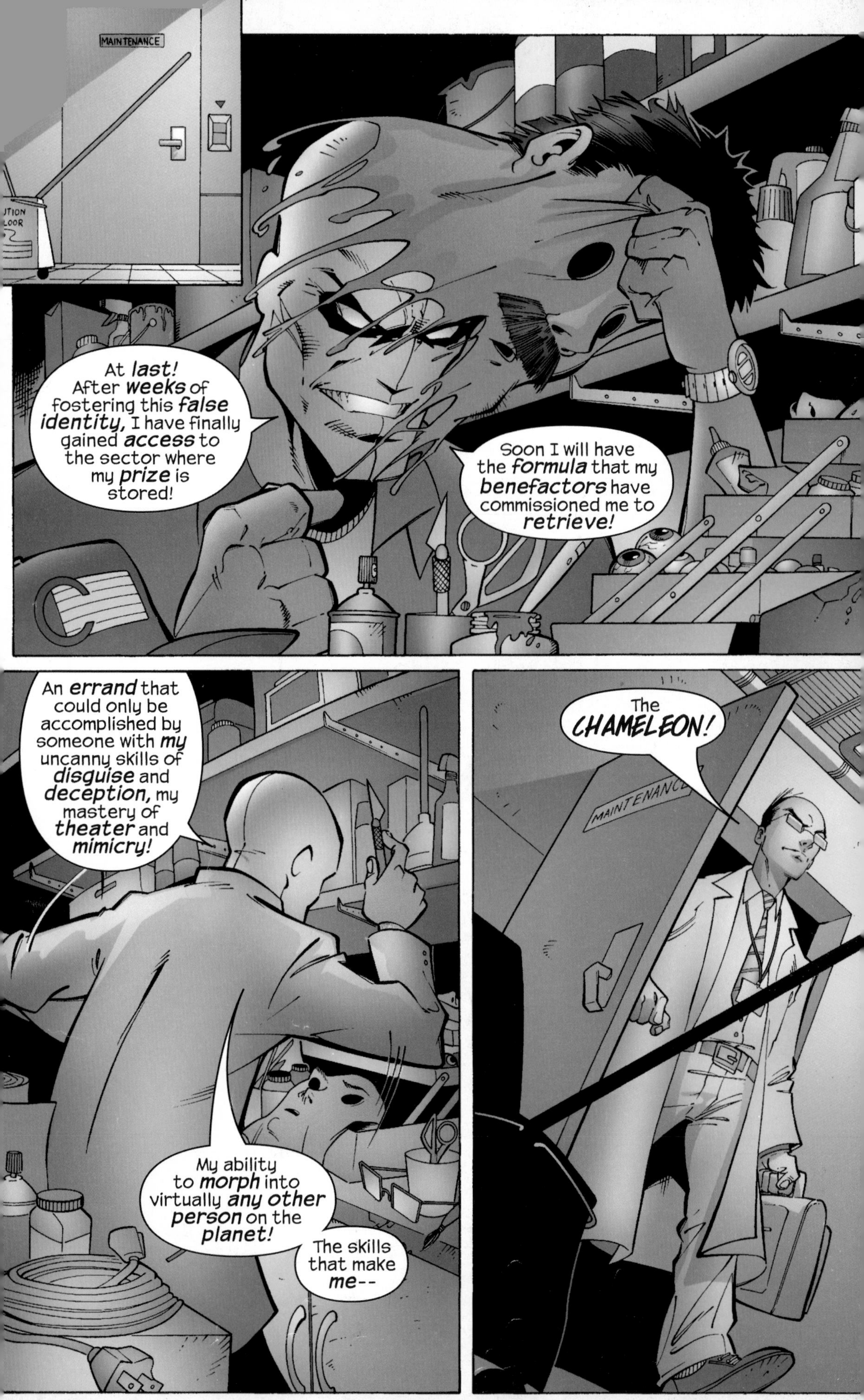
MAINTENANCE
At last! After weeks of fostering this false identity, I have finally gained access to the sector where my prize is stored!
Soon I will have the formula that my benefactors have commissioned me to retrieve!
An errand that could only be accomplished by someone with my uncanny skills of disguise and deception, my mastery of theater and mimicry!
My ability to morph into virtually any other person on the planet!
The skills that make me--
The CHAMELEON!
MAINTENANCE

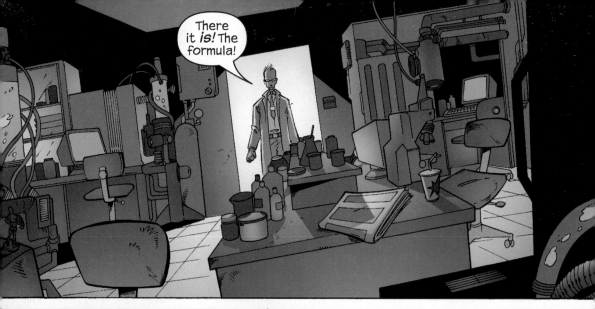

There it *is!* The formula!

Mine for the *taking!*

But *no!* My benefactors made it *clear* that this misappropriation was to be *clean*--there can be *no chance* of this job being *traced* back to *them...* or me...

And as good as I *am*, too many of my *associates* in the *spying* community would see my *finger-prints* all over this...

No, I decided long ago that I would need a *fall guy* to take the *blame* for this theft. But there's *no one* who could possibly be considered a viable--

Ah, *wait...*

...maybe there *is!*

DAILY BUGLE

NEW YORK'S FINEST DAILY NEWSPAPER

ER-MAN MENACES SCHOOL

Partly cl...

Kid: *Look*, Mom! It's *Spider-Man!*

Mom: *Oh my!*

Man: *Daily Bugle* says he's a--

Spider-Man: --menace!

Spider-Man: Don't believe everything you *read*, folks! I'm more like an *obnoxious prankster.*

Really. I'm a very nice *person.*

Spider-Man: *Hello!* The *Amazing, Spectacular,* and *Sensational* Spider-Man to see the Fantastic Four!

You can use any *one* of those adjectives...

...or, why not use them all!

Receptionist: And do you have an *appointment,* Mr. Man?

Spider-Man: Ummm, no. But I'm a fairly *popular* super hero. Isn't there *some* way you could just...*buzz* me up?

Receptionist: I'm sorry, but security precautions *prohibit* my letting you in without *prior* authorization.

Spider-Man: Yeah, but there's gotta be *some* way to get *around* all that...

Receptionist: Our security system was designed by Reed Richards *himself.* To successfully *circumvent* it would be an *impressive* feat indeed.

Spider-Man: Hmmmm. It *would,* wouldn't it...?

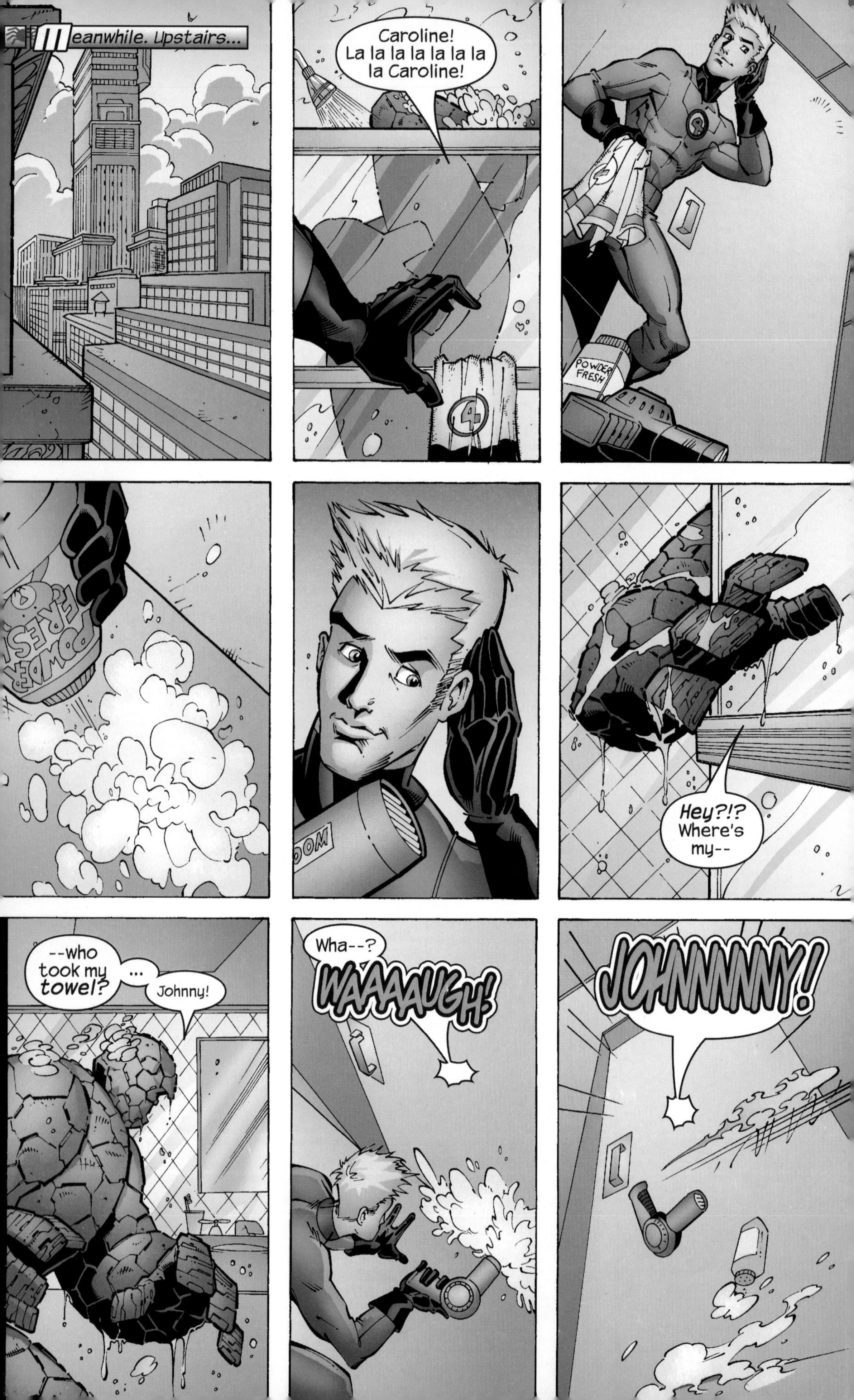
Meanwhile. Upstairs...
Caroline! La la la la la la la la Caroline!
POWDER FRESH
DOOM
Hey?!? Where's my--
--who took my towel?
...
Johnny!
Wha--?
WAAAAUGH!
JOHNNNNNY!

Okay, Sue. Now see if you can slowly return to the *visible spectrum...*

How's that?

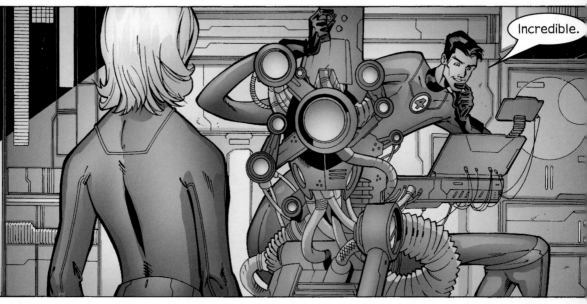

Incredible.

I'd take that as a *compliment,* Dr. Richards, if I could only be certain that you were referring to my *stunning beauty*--

--and *not* my ability to "manipulate *light waves* to render myself invisible."

Definitely the *former,* Miss Storm.

Although you should see what I was able to capture this time through the *micro-spectra-scope!*

Now I know you say that your inner trigger is more of an *emotional response,* but in *technical* terms the *process* is...

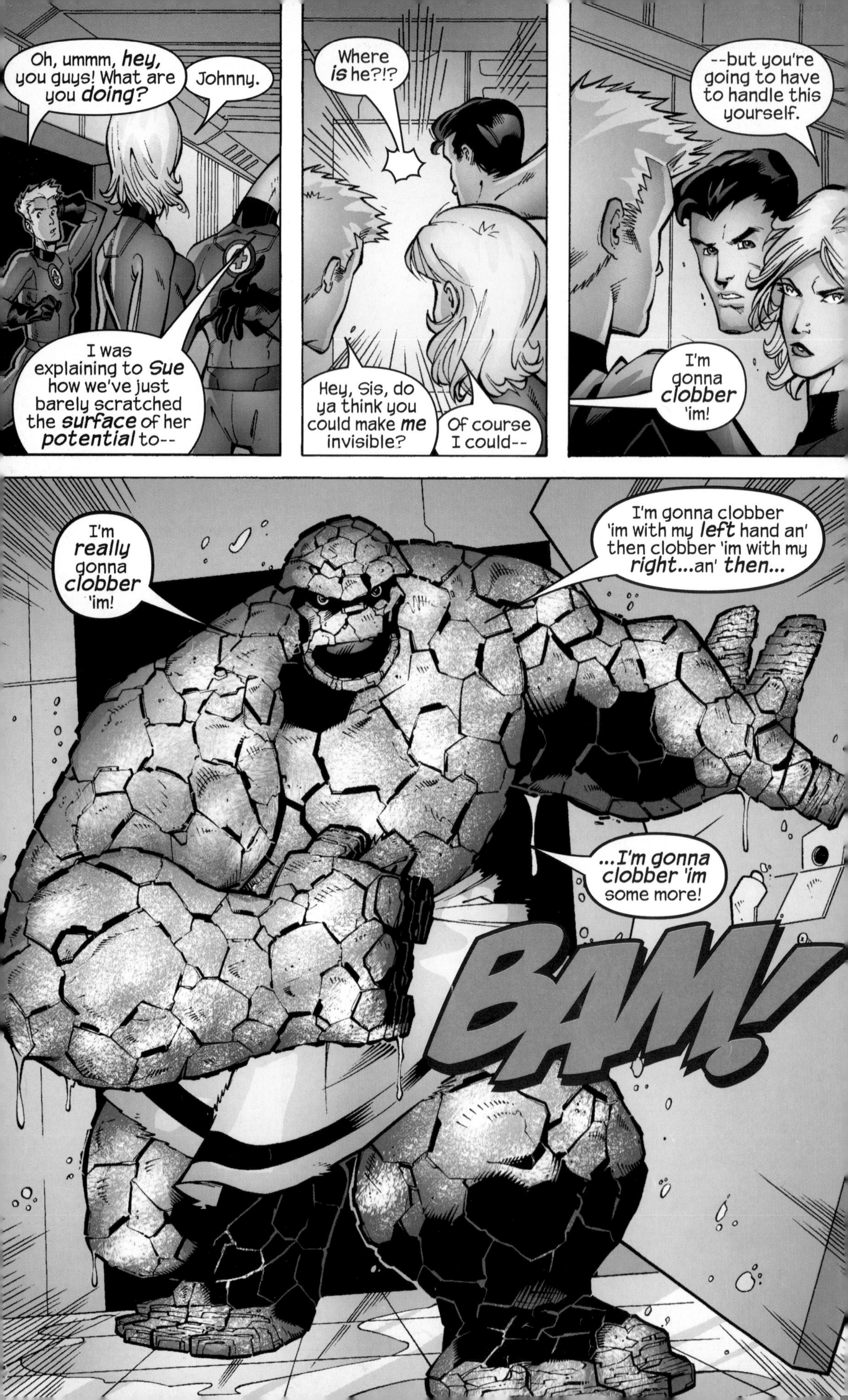
Oh, ummm, hey, you guys! What are you doing?
Johnny.
I was explaining to Sue how we've just barely scratched the surface of her potential to--
Where is he?!?
Hey, Sis, do ya think you could make me invisible?
Of course I could--
--but you're going to have to handle this yourself.
I'm gonna clobber 'im!
I'm really gonna clobber 'im!
I'm gonna clobber 'im with my left hand an' then clobber 'im with my right...an' then...
...I'm gonna clobber 'im some more!
BAM!

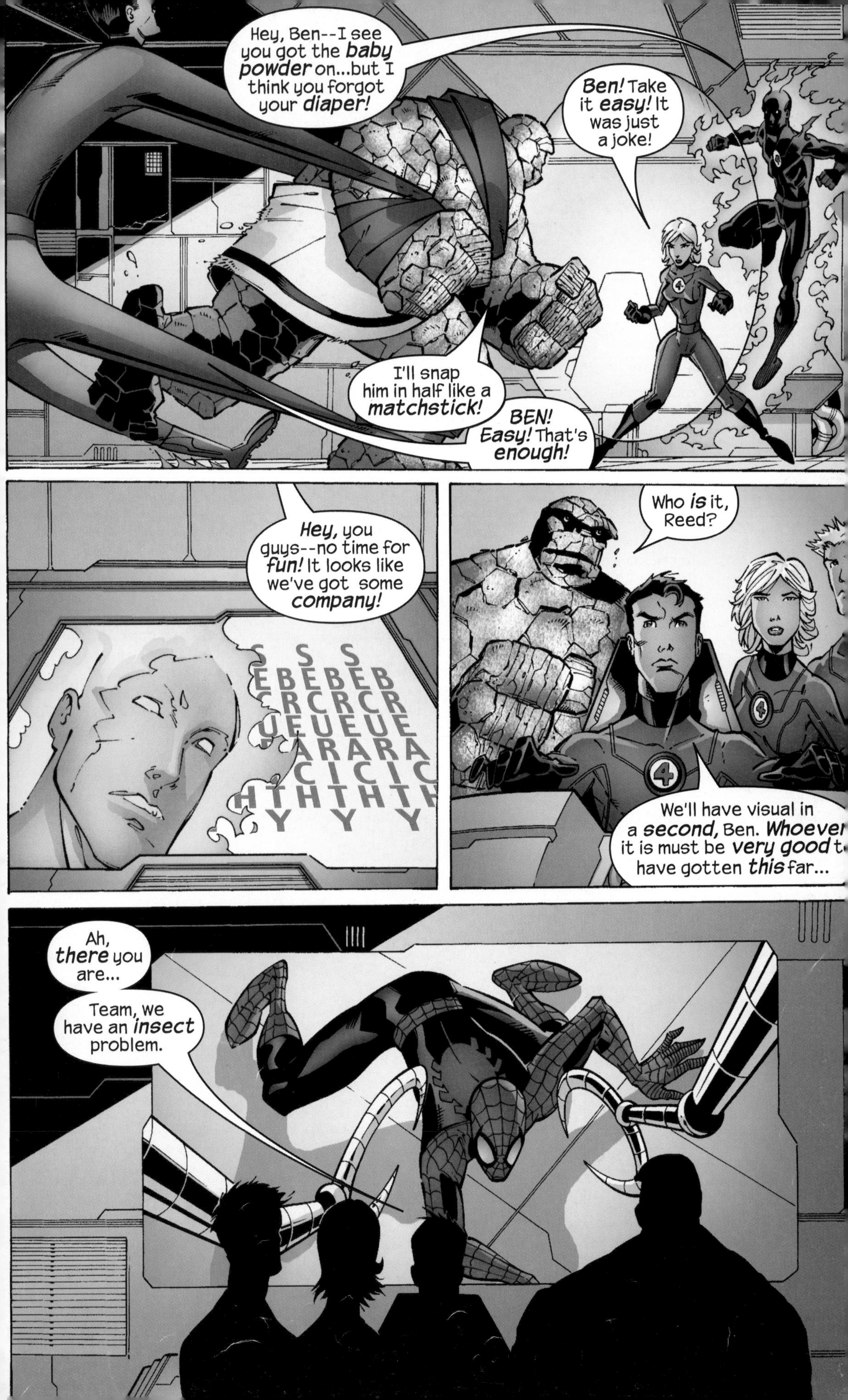
Hey, Ben--I see you got the baby powder on...but I think you forgot your diaper!
Ben! Take it easy! It was just a joke!
I'll snap him in half like a matchstick!
BEN! Easy! That's enough!
Hey, you guys--no time for fun! It looks like we've got some company!
SECURITY SECURITY SECURITY
Who is it, Reed?
We'll have visual in a second, Ben. Whoever it is must be very good to have gotten this far...
Ah, there you are...
Team, we have an insect problem.

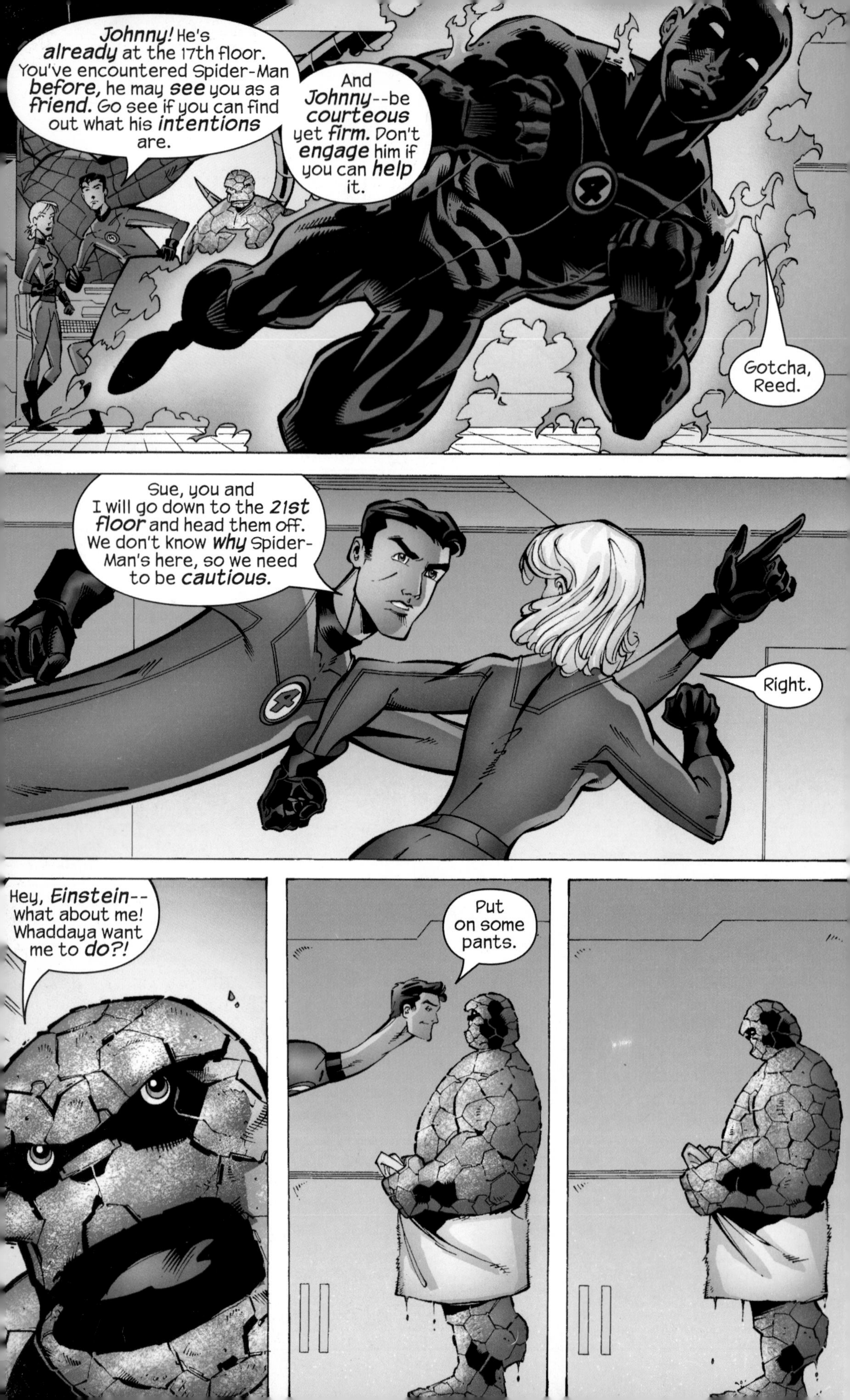
Johnny! He's already at the 17th floor. You've encountered Spider-Man before, he may see you as a friend. Go see if you can find out what his intentions are.
And Johnny--be courteous yet firm. Don't engage him if you can help it.
Gotcha, Reed.
Sue, you and I will go down to the 21st floor and head them off. We don't know why Spider-Man's here, so we need to be cautious.
Right.
Hey, Einstein--what about me! Whaddaya want me to do?!
Put on some pants.

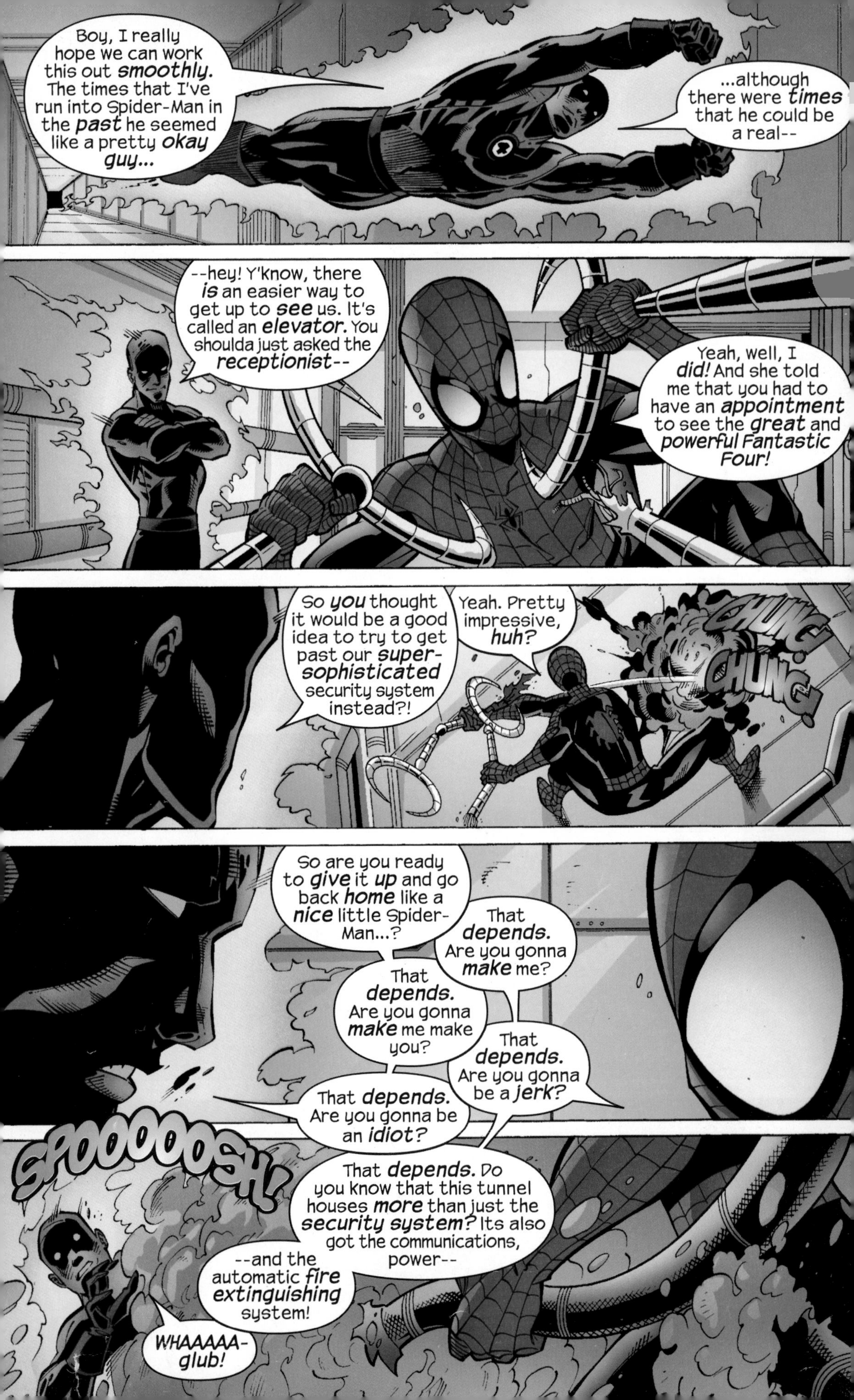
Boy, I really hope we can work this out smoothly. The times that I've run into Spider-Man in the past he seemed like a pretty okay guy...
...although there were times that he could be a real--
--hey! Y'know, there is an easier way to get up to see us. It's called an elevator. You shoulda just asked the receptionist--
Yeah, well, I did! And she told me that you had to have an appointment to see the great and powerful Fantastic Four!
So you thought it would be a good idea to try to get past our super-sophisticated security system instead?!
Yeah. Pretty impressive, huh?
CHUNG
CHUNG
So are you ready to give it up and go back home like a nice little Spider-Man...?
That depends. Are you gonna make me?
That depends. Are you gonna make me make you?
That depends. Are you gonna be a jerk?
That depends. Are you gonna be an idiot?
SPOOOOOSH!
That depends. Do you know that this tunnel houses more than just the security system? Its also got the communications, power--
--and the automatic fire extinguishing system!
WHAAAAA-glub!

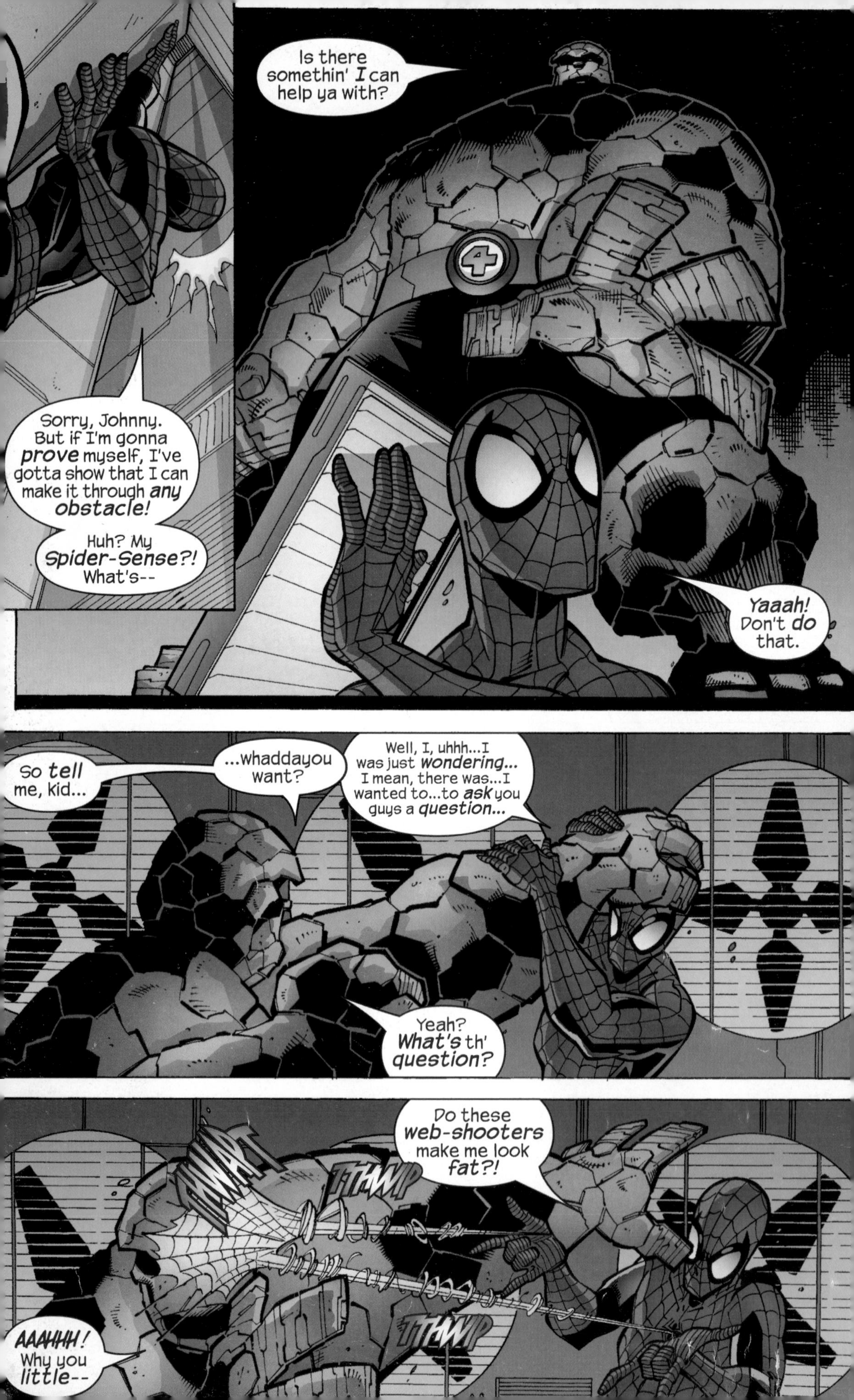
Is there somethin' I can help ya with?
Sorry, Johnny. But if I'm gonna prove myself, I've gotta show that I can make it through any obstacle!
Huh? My Spider-Sense?! What's--
Yaaah! Don't do that.
So tell me, kid...
...whaddayou want?
Well, I, uhhh...I was just wondering... I mean, there was...I wanted to...to ask you guys a question...
Yeah? What's th' question?
Do these web-shooters make me look fat?!
THWIP
THWIP
AAAHHH! Why you little--

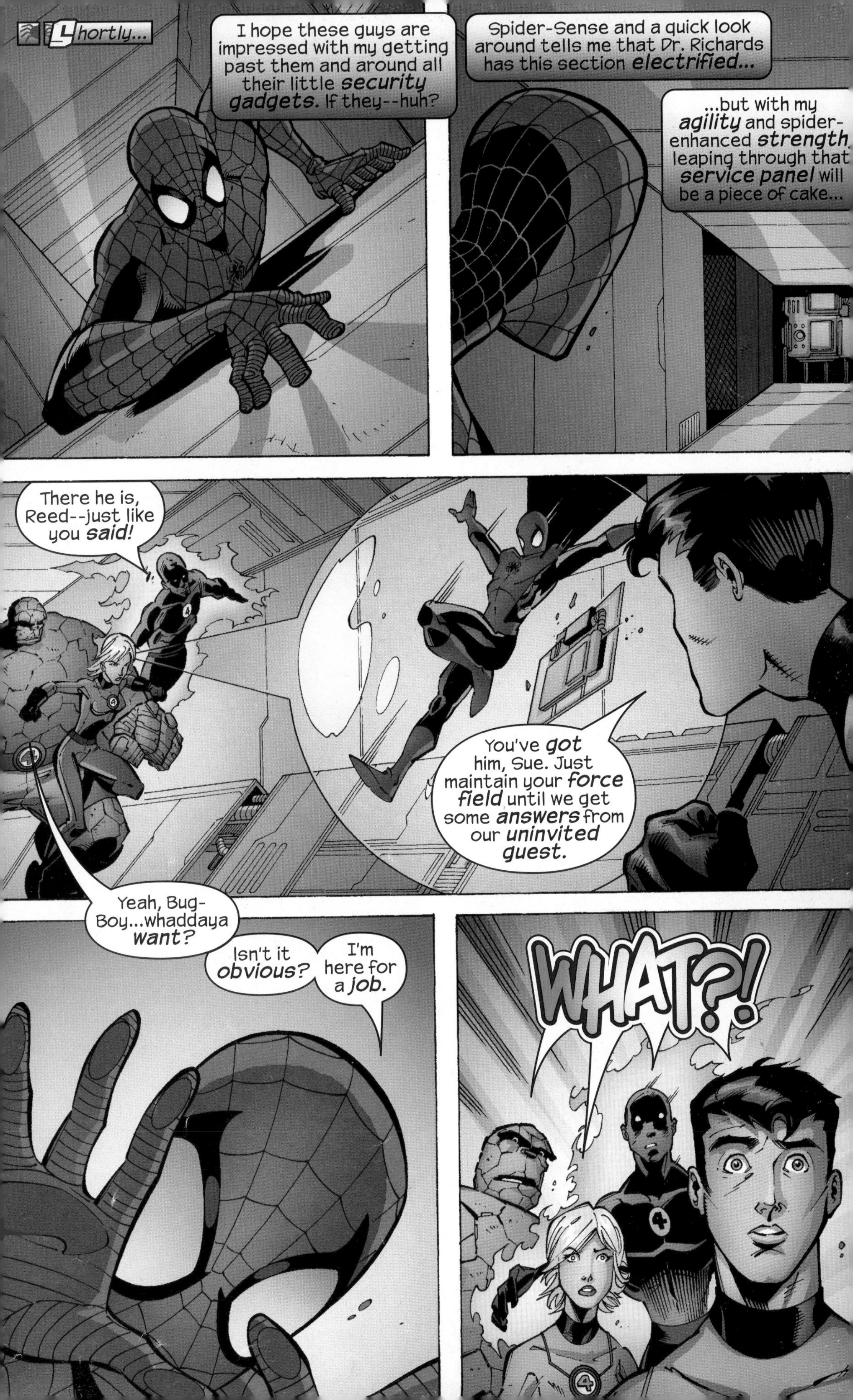
Shortly...
I hope these guys are impressed with my getting past them and around all their little security gadgets. If they--huh?
Spider-Sense and a quick look around tells me that Dr. Richards has this section electrified...
...but with my agility and spider-enhanced strength, leaping through that service panel will be a piece of cake...
There he is, Reed--just like you said!
You've got him, Sue. Just maintain your force field until we get some answers from our uninvited guest.
Yeah, Bug-Boy...whaddaya want?
Isn't it obvious?
I'm here for a job.
WHAT?!

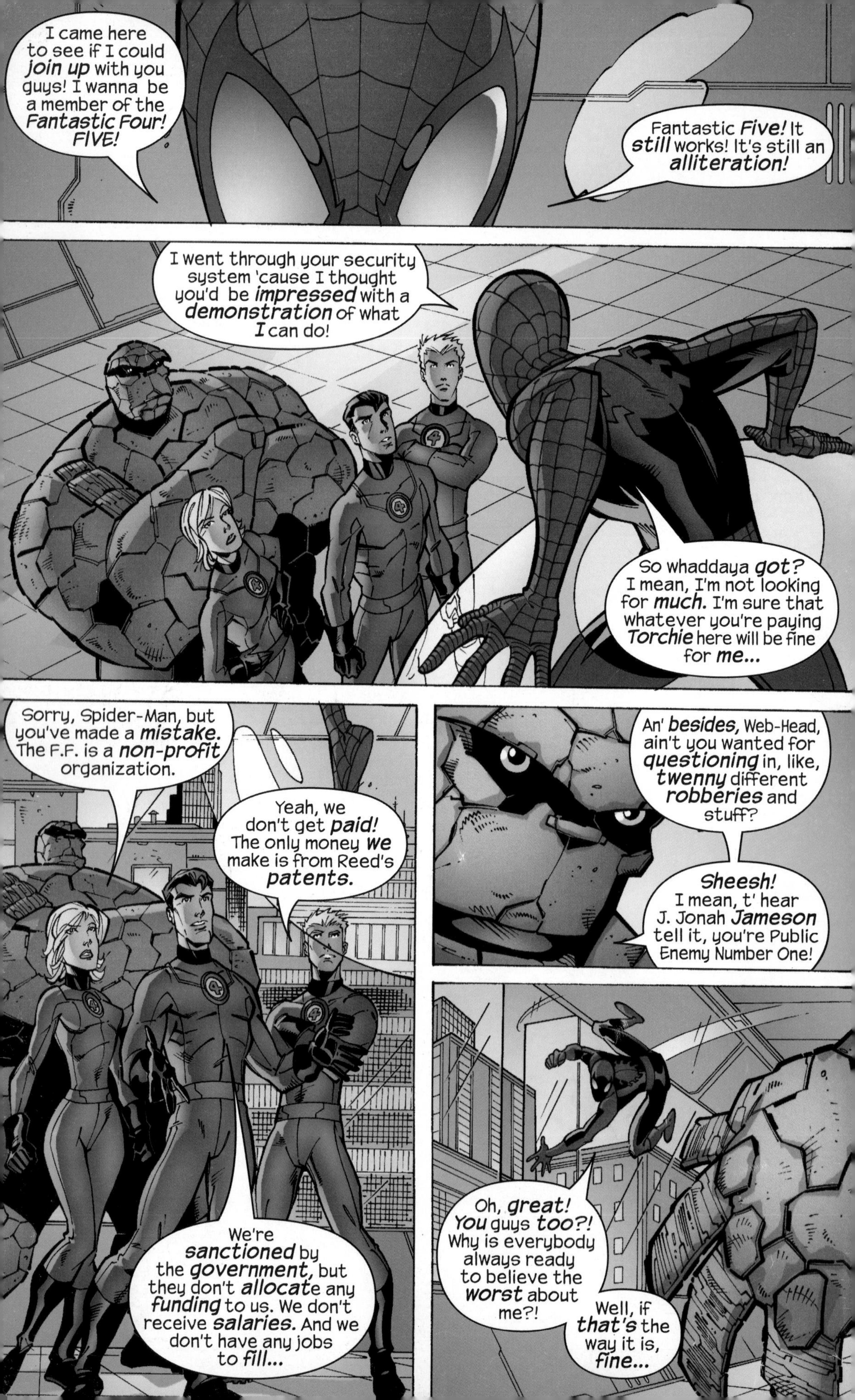
I came here to see if I could *join up* with you guys! I wanna be a member of the *Fantastic Four! FIVE!*
Fantastic *Five!* It *still* works! It's still an *alliteration!*
I went through your security system 'cause I thought you'd be *impressed* with a *demonstration* of what *I* can do!
So whaddaya *got?* I mean, I'm not looking for *much*. I'm sure that whatever you're paying *Torchie* here will be fine for *me...*
Sorry, Spider-Man, but you've made a *mistake*. The F.F. is a *non-profit* organization.
Yeah, we don't get *paid!* The only money *we* make is from Reed's *patents.*
We're *sanctioned* by the *government,* but they don't *allocate* any *funding* to us. We don't receive *salaries.* And we don't have any jobs to *fill...*
An' *besides,* Web-Head, ain't you wanted for *questioning* in, like, *twenny* different *robberies* and stuff?
Sheesh! I mean, t' hear J. Jonah *Jameson* tell it, you're Public Enemy Number One!
Oh, *great! You* guys *too?!* Why is everybody always ready to believe the *worst* about me?!
Well, if *that's* the way it is, *fine...*

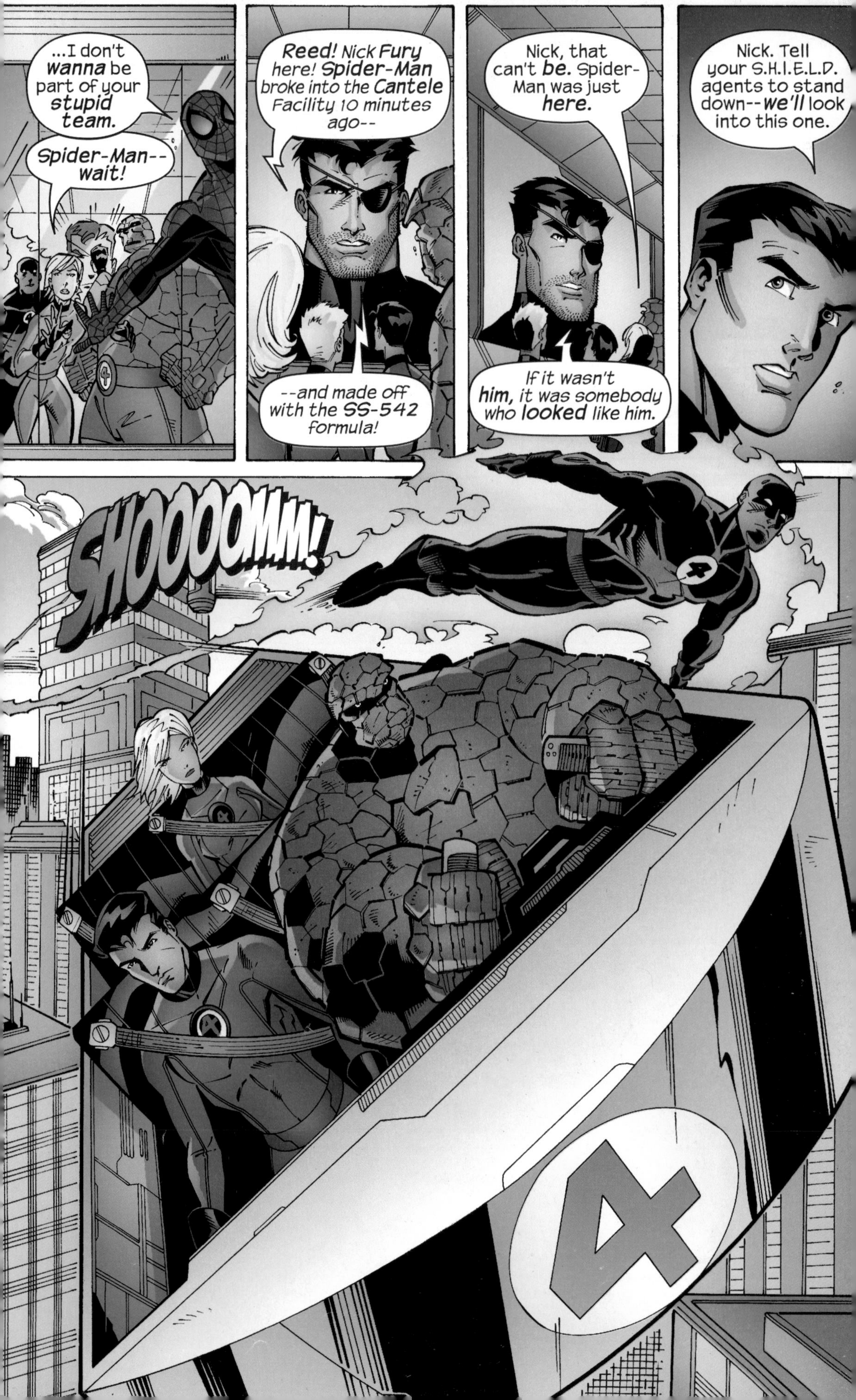
...I don't wanna be part of your stupid team.
Spider-Man-- wait!
Reed! Nick Fury here! Spider-Man broke into the Cantele Facility 10 minutes ago--
--and made off with the SS-542 formula!
Nick, that can't be. Spider-Man was just here.
If it wasn't him, it was somebody who looked like him.
Nick. Tell your S.H.I.E.L.D. agents to stand down--we'll look into this one.
SHOOOOMM!

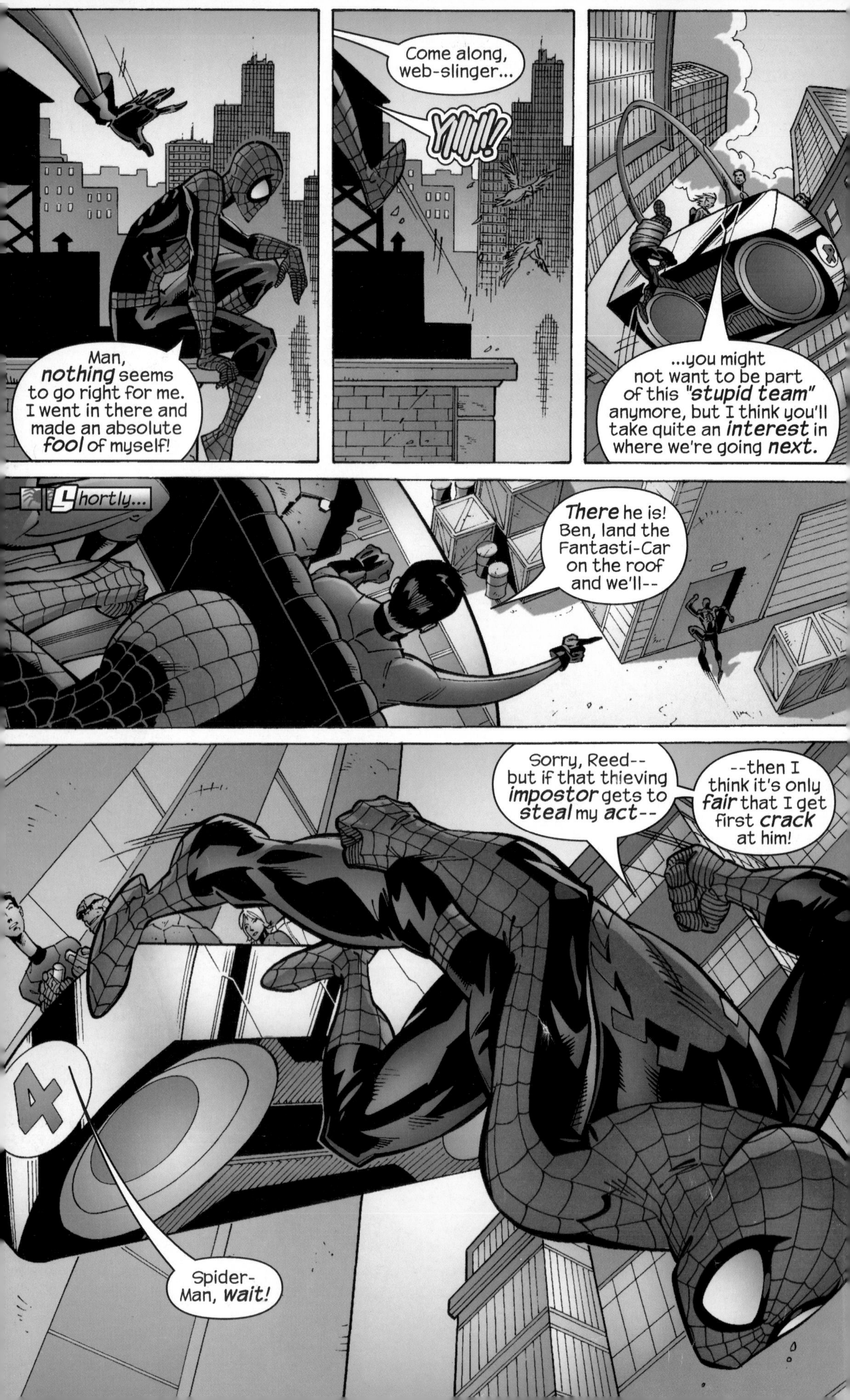
Man, nothing seems to go right for me. I went in there and made an absolute fool of myself!
Come along, web-slinger...
YIIII!
...you might not want to be part of this "stupid team" anymore, but I think you'll take quite an interest in where we're going next.
Shortly...
There he is! Ben, land the Fantasti-Car on the roof and we'll--
Sorry, Reed-- but if that thieving impostor gets to steal my act--
--then I think it's only fair that I get first crack at him!
Spider-Man, wait!

"We won't be able to tell the two of you *apart!*"

Y'know, you *see* those identity theft commercials on *TV,* but you just *never think* that it could happen to *you...*

Uh... uh...

Oh, you'd *better* run! When I catch up to *you,* I'm gonna--

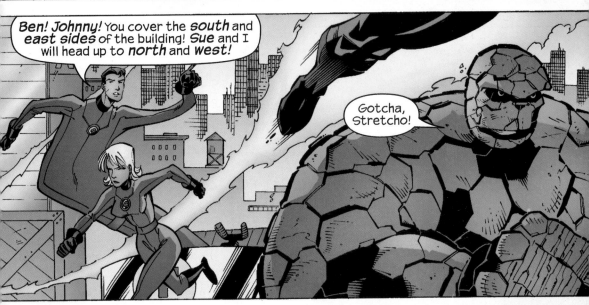

Ben! Johnny! You cover the *south* and *east sides* of the building! *Sue* and I will head up to *north* and *west!*

Gotcha, Stretcho!

He's right...⟨huff huff⟩...*behind* me! But I can't go *on*...have to *hide*...and hope he believes that I...⟨huff huff⟩...continued on!

Typical, Spidey. Now you've *lost* the jerk! You shouldn't have given him such a big *head sta--*

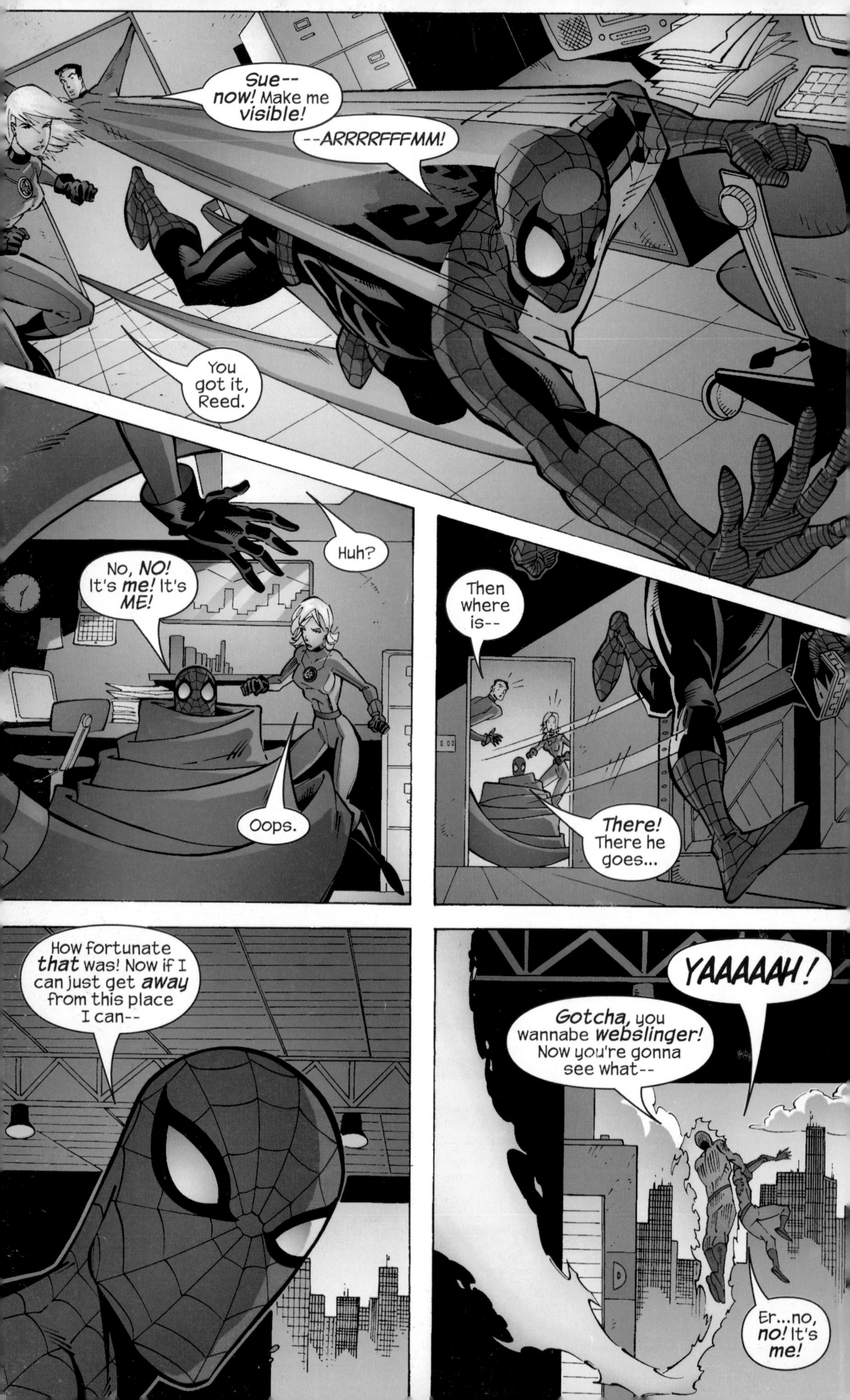

Sue-- now! Make me visible!
--ARRRRFFFMM!
You got it, Reed.
Huh?
No, NO! It's me! It's ME!
Oops.
Then where is--
There! There he goes...
How fortunate that was! Now if I can just get away from this place I can--
YAAAAAH!
Gotcha, you wannabe webslinger! Now you're gonna see what--
Er...no, no! It's me!

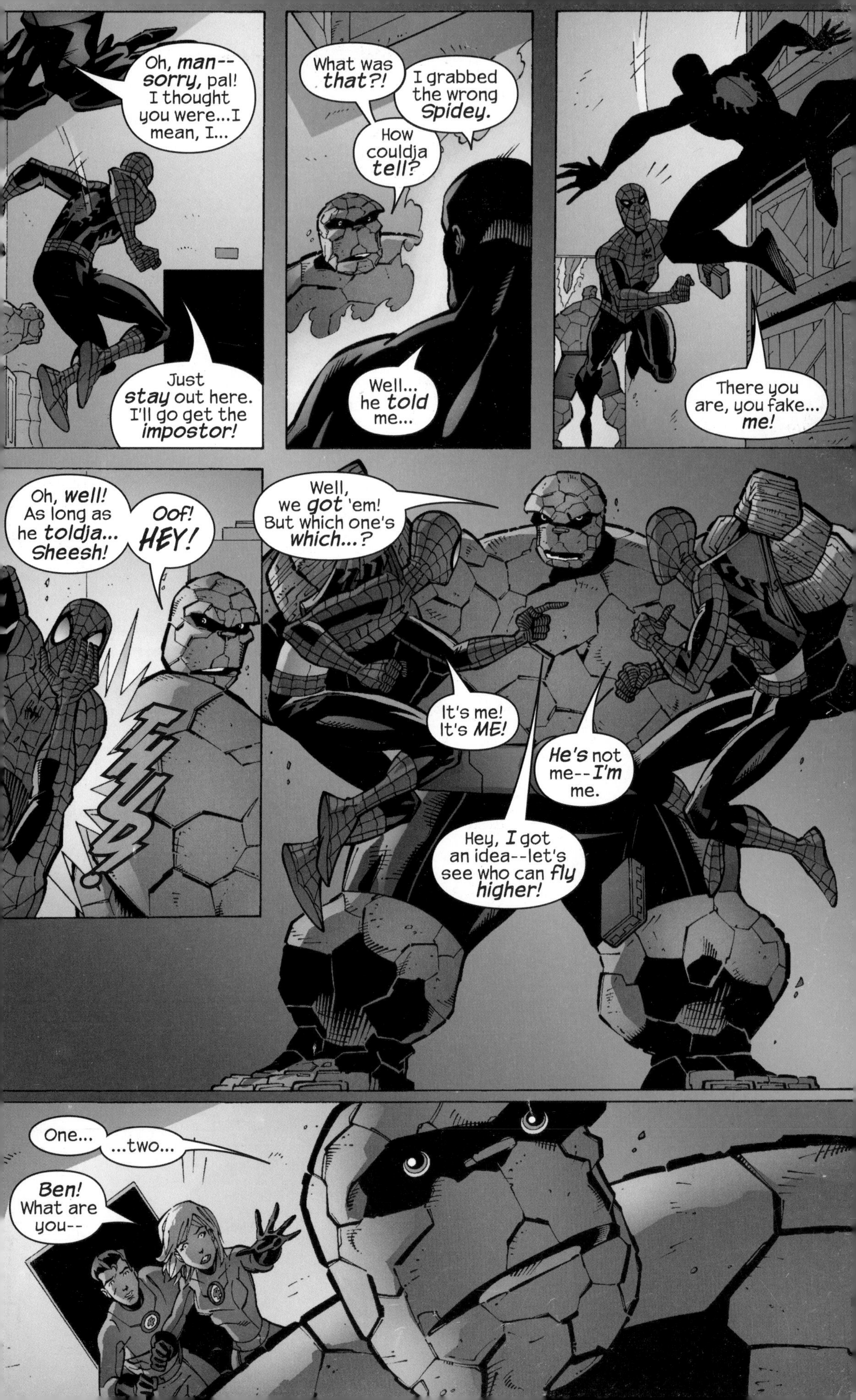
Oh, man--
sorry, pal! I thought you were...I mean, I...
Just stay out here. I'll go get the impostor!
What was that?!
I grabbed the wrong Spidey.
How couldja tell?
Well... he told me...
There you are, you fake... me!
Oh, well! As long as he toldja... Sheesh!
Oof! HEY!
THUD!
Well, we got 'em! But which one's which...?
It's me! It's ME!
He's not me--I'm me.
Hey, I got an idea--let's see who can fly higher!
One...
...two...
Ben! What are you--

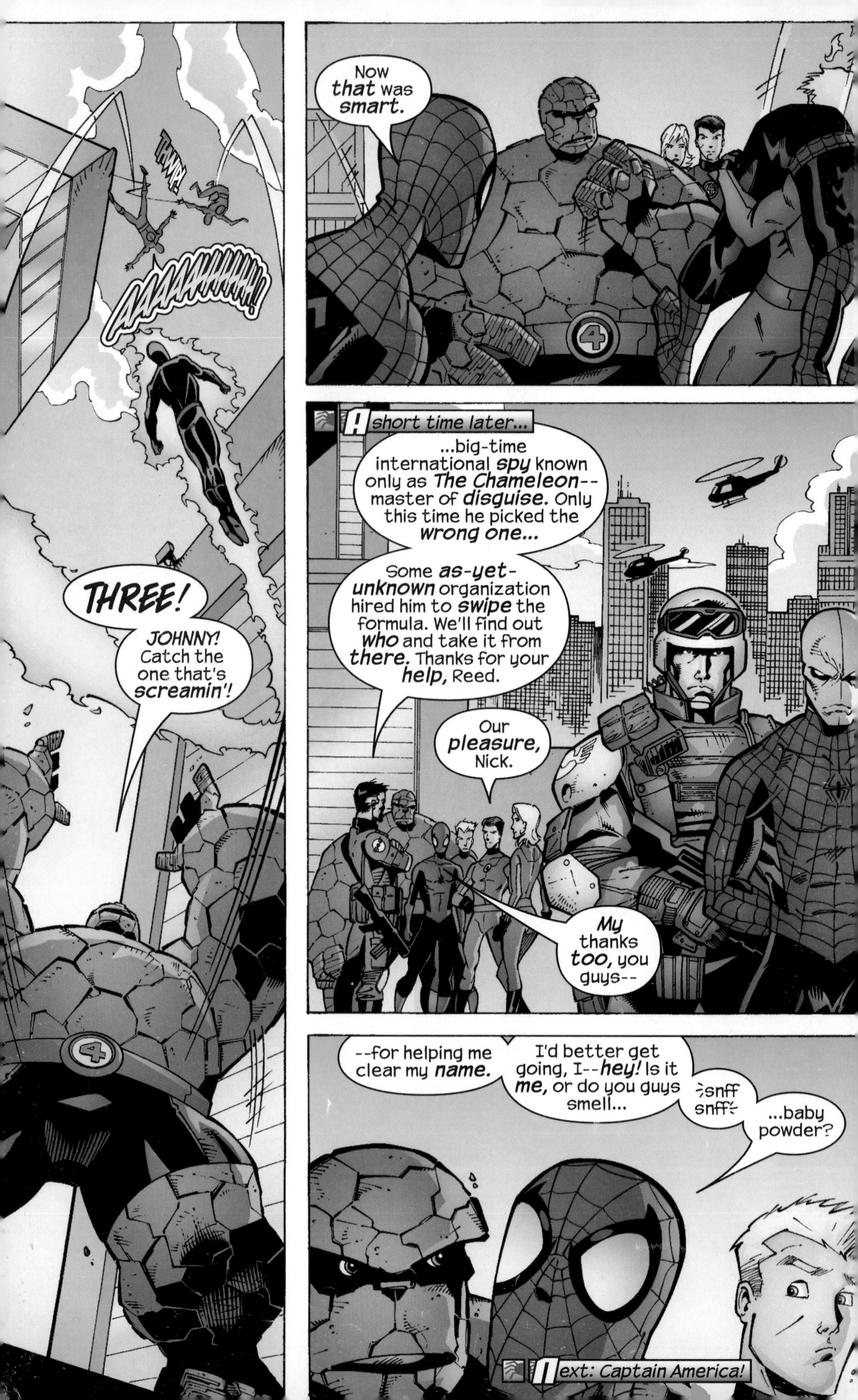
THWIP!
AAAAAHHHHH!
THREE!
JOHNNY! Catch the one that's screamin'!
Now that was smart.
A short time later...
...big-time international spy known only as The Chameleon--master of disguise. Only this time he picked the wrong one...
Some as-yet-unknown organization hired him to swipe the formula. We'll find out who and take it from there. Thanks for your help, Reed.
Our pleasure, Nick.
My thanks too, you guys--
--for helping me clear my name.
I'd better get going, I--hey! Is it me, or do you guys smell...
snff snff
...baby powder?
Next: Captain America!